Published in the United States by Random House Children's Books, a division of Penguin Random House LLC, 1745 Broadway, New York, NY 10019, and in Canada by Penguin Random House Canada Limited, Toronto.
Random House and the colophon are registered trademarks of Penguin Random House LLC.
ISBN 978-0-593-42529-9 (trade) — ISBN 978-0-593-42530-5 (ebook)
MANUFACTURED IN CHINA
10 9 8 7 6 5 4 3 2 1

Let's All Sing Together!

A Celebration of Our Differences

By Megan Roth
Illustrated by Gladys Jose

Random House New York

Each Troll's voice is different.
All Trolls have their very own sound.
But when we join together,
our toes start tappin' on the ground.

TROLLS KINGDOM
VIBE CITY
RIVER
TROLLS VILLAGE
MOUNTAINS
TECHNO REEF

Some can't stop playing
unforgettable chords,
for that fun, repeatable hook,

while others compose
sweet, dazzling scores
in their classical music books.

Some of us play elegant sounds
to the swishing of a baton,

while others get hyped up to dance,
knowing the beat will go on and on!

Some of us jump up and down
as light shows fill the skies,

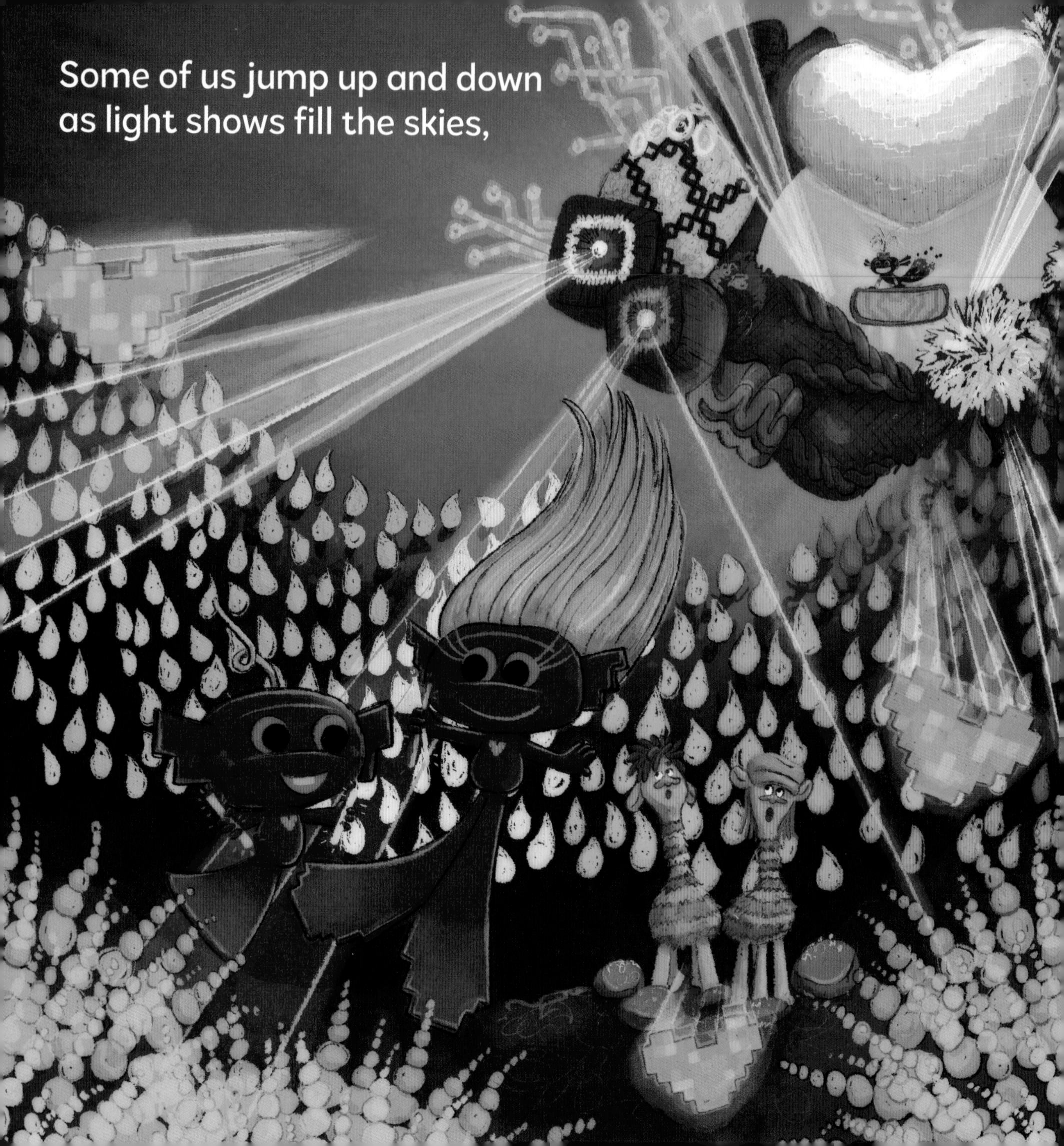

while others groove to funky beats
as stars dance in their eyes.

Some of us sing out low, slow notes
as we roast s’mores ’round a fire,

while others jam to rock ’n’ roll
as hard as their hearts desire.

Some Trolls shred with all six strings
on extra-loud guitars,

while some Trolls sing soft melodies
for no one but the stars.

Some of us long for rainy days
so we can play the blues,

while others chase the rain away
with pop-and-lock dance moves!

Some of us start to shake and slide
when we hear that K-Pop beat,

while others hear sweet yodeling
and keep time with their feet.

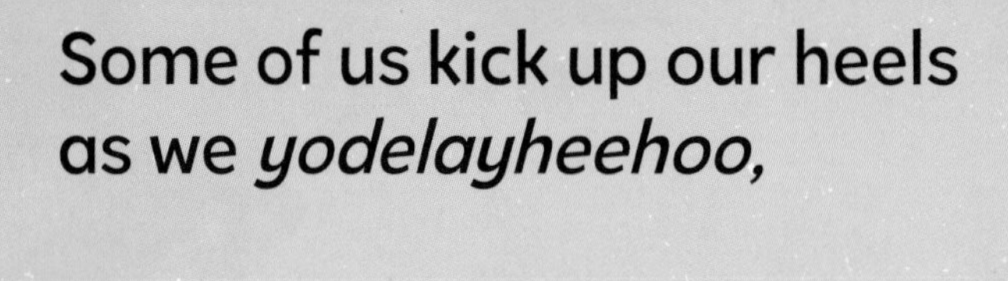

Some of us kick up our heels
as we *yodelayheehoo,*

and others sing while standing still—
so they don't mess up their 'dos!

Some of us crank a country twang
in a honky-tonk full of friends,

while others choose fresh blended beats
for a party that never ends.

Our harmonies may flow differently,
but we're thankful for what each Troll brings,

because that's what helps us all come up with even more awesome songs to sing!

We love that each Troll is different.
It's what makes life so much fun.
So we celebrate each other—
and we've only just begun!